Franklin and the Baby

From an episode of the animated TV series *Franklin* produced by Nelvana Limited, Neurones France s.a.r.l. and Neurones Luxembourg S.A.

Based on the *Franklin* books by Paulette Bourgeois and Brenda Clark.

TV tie-in adaptation written by Eva Moore and illustrated by Nelvana.
TV script written by Bonnie Chung.

Franklin is a trade mark of Kids Can Press Ltd.
Kids Can Press is a Nelvana Company.

ISBN 0-439-12065-9

12 11 10 9 8 7 6 5 4 3 2   9/9 0 1 2 3 4/0

Printed in the U.S.A.

First Scholastic printing, November 1999

Franklin and the Baby

Based on the characters created by
Paulette Bourgeois and Brenda Clark

SCHOLASTIC INC.

New York   Toronto   London   Auckland   Sydney
Mexico City   New Delhi   Hong Kong

FRANKLIN was a son, a grandson, and a nephew. But he was not a brother. Franklin often thought about being a big brother, and he wondered what it would be like to have a baby in the family. Franklin was going to find out soon because his best friend, Bear, was about to become a big brother.

One day Franklin was having lunch with Bear and Snail. Bear had two lunch boxes filled with cookies, muffins, and brownies.

"Wow, Bear!" said Franklin. "Your lunch looks good."

"I packed it myself," said Bear.

Franklin was surprised.

"My mom and dad were busy putting the crib together," Bear explained. "I made my own breakfast, too. When you're a big brother, you've got to do more things for yourself."

"Are you a big brother now?" Franklin asked.

"Not yet, but I will be soon," said Bear.

"Are you excited?" asked Snail.

"I sure am," Bear answered. "My dad says that when the baby gets too big for the crib, we might get bunk beds!"

Franklin thought Bear was lucky.

The next day at school, Bear was still talking about the baby.

"I get to stay at Franklin's house when the baby is ready to be born," he told Snail.

"A sleepover!" Snail cried. "I wish *my* mom were having a baby."

"Me, too," said Franklin. "When you're a big brother, you've got someone to play with all the time."

"Yes," said Bear, "it's going to be fun!"

After school Franklin's mother was
waiting at the bus stop.

"Why are you carrying that pillow?"
Franklin asked her.

"This is Bear's pillow," she replied.
"Guess who's sleeping at our house tonight?"

Bear's eyes lit up. "Is the baby ready to
be born?"

Franklin's mother nodded.

"Hooray!" cried Franklin and Bear. "The baby is coming!"

Franklin's mother asked Bear what he would like for supper. Bear could hardly believe his good luck.

"I'm going to be a big brother. I'm sleeping over at my best friend's house. And I'm having pancakes with blueberries!"

Franklin was happy, too. But he couldn't help feeling a little jealous.

"Gee," he said, "lots of good things happen when you're a big brother."

Franklin and Bear stayed up long past their bedtime. They made up a puppet play about a big brother who rescues his baby brother from a dragon's cave. Bear played the big brother, and Franklin played the dragon.

They tried to fall asleep, but they were still awake when Franklin's parents came in to tell them the big news.

"Bear, you have a brand-new baby sister!" announced Franklin's mother.

"Wow! Now you really are a big brother," said Franklin.

Bear looked as if he would burst with pride. "This is my best day ever!" he said.

A few days later Franklin walked over to Bear's
house. He found Bear sitting on the front steps.

"Why aren't you playing with your sister?"
asked Franklin.

"She's too little, and she sleeps all the time,"
sighed Bear. "Being a big brother isn't as much fun
as I thought it would be."

Franklin was surprised. "Could I see her?"
he asked.

"Only if you promise to be quiet," Bear replied.
"I'm not supposed to go into her room when she's
sleeping."

Franklin promised not to make a single sound.

Bear led Franklin to his sister's room, and they
tiptoed to the crib.

The baby was fast asleep.

Franklin thought she looked small and smelled nice.

"Oh," he whispered. "What does this toy do?"

Franklin reached up and touched the mobile above
the crib. It began to whirl around and play a tune.

"Oh, no," said Bear. "She's going to wake up!"

Bear's baby sister opened one eye, then the other.

"Please don't cry," Bear whispered.

The baby blinked and took a deep breath. "Waaaaaaa," she wailed.

Franklin looked alarmed.

"Let's go," said Bear.

But they didn't get far. Bear's mother met them at the door.

"What are you two doing in here?" she asked.

"I just wanted to show Franklin the baby," Bear answered.

"I understand," said Bear's mother, "but we should try not to disturb her when she's asleep."

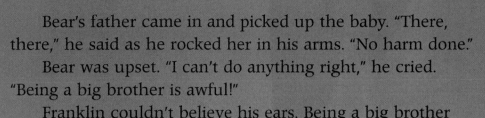

Bear's father came in and picked up the baby. "There, there," he said as he rocked her in his arms. "No harm done."

Bear was upset. "I can't do anything right," he cried. "Being a big brother is awful!"

Franklin couldn't believe his ears. Being a big brother was supposed to be special.

Bear looked at his parents. "Since the baby came, you've forgotten all about me."

Bear's mother gave him a hug. "We would never forget you, Bear. But we have been busy," she explained. "Babies need a lot of attention."

"You did, too, when you were a baby," his father added.

"Did I cry all the time like she does?" Bear asked.

"Yes," his mother replied. "All babies do. That's how they tell their families that they need something."

"In a few weeks, she'll be crying to see her big brother," said Bear's father. "You'll see."

"Really?" said Bear. The idea made him smile.

The next time Franklin visited Bear, things were different. When his sister began to cry, Bear picked up her rattle and shook it. The baby stopped crying and began cooing softly.

"A lot of the time, she cries because she wants to play," Bear told him, "so I shake the rattle or give her a toy."

"You sure know a lot about babies," said Franklin.

"Would you like to hold the baby, Franklin?" asked Bear's father.

"Could I?" said Franklin.

Franklin sat in the rocking chair and held his breath as Bear's father placed the baby in his arms. Bear showed him just how to hold her.

Franklin held the baby gently for a few minutes.

"Bear, I really like your baby sister," he said.

The baby smiled at Franklin.

"She likes you, too," said Bear. "You're my best friend. That makes you her best-friend brother."

Franklin thought that being a best-friend brother was almost like being a big brother—and just as special.